Princess Poppy
Ballet Dreams

Check out Princess Poppy's website
to find out all about the other
books in the series

www.princesspoppy.com

Princess Poppy
Ballet Dreams

written by Janey Louise Jones
Illustrated by Samantha Chaffey

YOUNG CORGI

BALLET DREAMS
A YOUNG CORGI BOOK 978 0 552 **56088** 7

Published in Great Britain by Young Corgi,
an imprint of Random House Children's Books
A Random House Group Company

This edition published 2008

1 3 5 7 9 10 8 6 4 2

Text copyright © Janey Louise Jones, 2008
Illustrations copyright © Random House Children's Books, 2008
Illustrated by Samantha Chaffey

The Random House Group Limited supports The Forest Stewardship
Council (FSC), the leading international forest certification organisation.
All our titles that are printed on Greenpeace approved FSC certified paper
carry the FSC logo. Our paper procurement policy can be found at
www.rbooks.co.uk/environment

Set in 14/20pt Bembo MT Schoolbook by
Falcon Oast Graphic Art Ltd.

Young Corgi Books are published by Random House Children's Books,
61–63 Uxbridge Road, London W5 5SA

www.princesspoppy.com
www.rbooks.co.uk

Addresses for companies within The Random House Group Limited can be
found at: www.randomhouse.co.uk/offices.htm

THE RANDOM HOUSE GROUP Limited Reg. No. 954009

A CIP catalogue record for this book is available from the British Library.

Printed and bound in Great Britain by CPI Bookmarque, Croydon, CR0 4TD

For Isabelle and Susanna, with love

Chapter One

Poppy always got butterflies in her tummy when her ballet exam was coming up. Her ballet teacher, Madame Angelwing, was always very demanding and ambitious for her girls, but at exam time she really wanted her little ballerinas to perform brilliantly. It was only eight weeks until Lady Margery de Mille, the examiner from the Royal Academy, would come to the Lavender Lake School of Dance to test Poppy and her friends.

One Tuesday, at the end of the weekly

ballet class, Madame Angelwing gave all the girls an information sheet about the exam and then talked them through it.

✦ INSTRUCTIONS FOR EXAMS:
ROYAL ACADEMY BALLET BOARD

Date of examination: Thursday, November 14th
Time: 4.45 p.m. Arrive at 4 p.m. sharp

Clothes: Please purchase outfits from Ballet Belles in the City, in pink, white, blue or lilac. Leotard, tights, tutu, ballet slippers, ribbons and a cardigan. Bring to the studio on the Tuesday before the exam to avoid costume problems on the day. Buy as soon as possible to avoid a poor selection, as the whole region is being examined at the same time and there will be a great demand.

Grade: Grade 1.
Possible results: Honours, Highly Commended,
                       Commended, Pass, Fail.

Length of exam: 20 minutes
Preparation: Tuesday class each week
                       and ten minutes' practice
                       twice a day.

Cost: £5.00.

Please see Madame Angelwing
with any further enquiries.

The girls folded the notes into their ballet cases.

"Don't forget to give them to your parents when you get home," said Madame Angelwing, "and, Honey, you give yours to your grandmother. Bye, girls!"

"Goodbye, Madame, see you next week!" they called as they trouped out of the dance school.

Poppy and Honey were both very hungry and thirsty after class so they decided to go to Bumble Bees Teashop for a snack and a drink.

"Hello, girls!" called Granny Bumble as they arrived. "And how was ballet today?"

"Oh, Granny, it was so good," replied Honey breathlessly. "We learned some new steps and Madame Angelwing told us all about the exam. We're going to have to do so much practice for it."

"Well, as long as you don't let it take over your lives – there is more to life than ballet, you know," commented Granny Bumble.

"Yeah, I know, but I really, really love it, and Madame Angelwing says that I could be a proper ballerina one day if I work hard, and I want to get Honours in the exam. Oh, and Granny, another thing," continued Honey, "Madame Angelwing says that we need new ballet outfits for the exam – look, she's given us a list. She says that we have to get everything from Ballet Belles in the City. Can we meet all the ballet girls

and their mums this Saturday and go up on the train? Madame said that if we don't go soon, there will be nothing left for us!"

"Well, if everyone else is going, I suppose we'll have to!" agreed Granny, less than cheerfully. "I'll just phone Holly Mallow and see if she can work here on Saturday. Mind you, I don't see what's wrong with the ballet outfits you've all got already."

At the weekend Poppy, Honey, Sweetpea, Mimosa, Abigail, all their mums and Granny Bumble met at the Honeypot Hill Railway Station to go up to the beautiful ballet shop in the city.

"I want a pale pink ballet dress and matching crossover cardigan!" said Sweetpea as they all settled down in their seats.

"I want a pale blue set!" declared Mimosa.

"Wait and see what's available in your size!" said Mimosa's mum.

"Yes, girls, she's right," said Poppy's mum. "You mustn't go setting your heart on things and then being disappointed if you can't have them."

"I'm getting a white leotard with a lilac top," Honey announced.

"Madame Angelwing and her fancy ideas, indeed!" tutted Granny Bumble. "Costs a fortune and you've got plenty of perfectly respectable tutus in the cupboard at home!"

Before long the train arrived at their destination. Everyone clambered out and made their way to the main shopping district.

"Here's Ballet Belles!" called Poppy, recognizing the heavenly ballet shop she had visited a couple of times before with Mum.

Everyone followed her in. They had a lovely time in the ballet shop looking at the rows of shell-pink satin ballet shoes, some with points like the older girls wore, and rails of pastel-coloured ballet dresses. Poppy loved

all the other pretty accessories too, such as satin ballet cases with mirrors inside, ballerina jewel boxes, hair bands and ribbons. There were also shelves of books about ballet.

"Look at all these pretty swans!" said Poppy as she and Honey flicked through a beautifully illustrated book about *Swan Lake*. "One day that will be you, Honey," she said proudly, pointing to a picture of a ballerina floating through the air.

Honey smiled. She absolutely adored ballet and she really hoped that one day she *would* be a ballerina, just like Madame Angelwing had been.

An hour or so later, after much choosing and trying on of outfits, everyone eventually found something that was just perfect, so they made their purchases and decided to go to an outdoor café in the old flower market area. The girls feasted on chocolate-chip muffins and frothy strawberry milkshakes and the grown-ups had creamy lattes and chocolate shortcake. At tea time they made their way back to the railway station and boarded the homeward train, feeling tired after their exciting ballet day.

Next Tuesday at ballet, all the girls turned up with their new outfits in smart Ballet Belles bags, ready to show Madame Angelwing. They practised their jumps and spins as Madame looked at their dresses, shoes and ribbons and smiled her approval.

"My girls," she cried, "you will all look simply wonderful when Lady Margery comes! My own ballet troupe. All my dreams have come true! You are the most dedicated dancers I have ever taught."

At the end of the lesson Madame asked all Grade One girls to stay behind.

"Are we in trouble?" whispered Honey, feeling nervous as usual.

Poppy shrugged her shoulders. She didn't think they had been naughty but you could never tell what was going to annoy grown-ups.

"Girls. *My* girls," began Madame, sipping some peppermint tea from her delicate china cup, "I have something important to ask you."

The girls looked at her with wide eyes.

"I am very impressed by all of you," she continued. "You show such dedication to ballet and such style. I would like to discuss with your parents and guardians an idea that

I have. I want to give you all advanced ballet lessons, free of charge, so that you can develop further before the exam. One day some of you might even consider going to ballet school and becoming professional dancers!"

The girls beamed with pride.

"Would you like me to see if it is allowed? We could do this every Saturday morning. What do you say?"

"Yes, please, Madame!" chorused the girls, absolutely thrilled by the idea.

Chapter Two

Madame Angelwing had scarcely felt so
excited in her whole teaching career. This
particular group of girls were extra
enthusiastic, which made her fizz with pride.
She called all the parents that evening about
the extra lessons.

As they waited for the first extra class to
come round, all the girls became very
excited, especially Poppy and Honey, who
were both super-keen on ballet. Poppy and
Mum went to the local library and took out
several ballet books – Poppy had been

reading about ballet in bed every night that week. Honey simply couldn't wait. She adored Madame Angelwing because she always took very special care of her. Madame understood how it felt to be different. She had also been brought up by her grandmother. Honey had never felt really special until she started ballet, but now she had something to work towards, and in the days before the first extra class, she practised as often as she could. She was determined to be the star dancer.

The next Saturday morning arrived at last and Poppy, Honey and Sweetpea met at Honeysuckle Cottage and made their way over to the dance school together for their first extra lesson. As it turned out, even though they were expecting to meet the others in the dance studio, they were the only ones there. Mimosa couldn't go as she wanted to earn some extra pocket money by helping out around the hotel on

Saturday mornings. And Abigail had a piano lesson, which her father would not let her cancel or move, much to her disappointment.

Poppy and her two close friends, Honey and Sweetpea, had never had so much of Madame Angelwing's attention and were all keen to impress her. When she appeared in the studio, Poppy, who liked to amaze her teacher with ballet facts, danced over to her, bursting with information she had picked up from her library books.

"Did you know that *The Sleeping Beauty* was first performed as a ballet in 1889?" she said. "Mum and Dad took me to see it in

the City as a birthday treat last year. It was
amazing!"

"How very interesting, Mademoiselle
Poppy. Now, when I was a young ballerina,

we had to dance until our feet could dance
no more. I remember when I was dancing
Princess Aurora in *Sleeping Beauty* in
Paris . . ." said Madame Angelwing as she
recounted one of her tales from her
professional career, which the girls found
fascinating, especially when other ballerinas
wanted the roles that Madame alone had
been lucky enough to dance!

"As this is our first special lesson,"
Madame went on when she had finished her

story, "I thought we could begin with some jobs around the studio. This will give you a feel of what it is like to be part of a ballet troupe. You will appreciate the work of those who stitch and sew, but never get to take a bow. How would you like to help me tidy the costume room? It's in a dreadful muddle and, as you know, our Big Show will be the next thing on the calendar after the exams. If the costume room is tidy, what a difference it will make! I have invited Saffron from the Sewing Shop to join us, and we can repair some of the beautiful dresses in there. A hook and eye here, a fixed seam there, and they will be as good as new again."

"Wow!" said Poppy. "Cool!"

Sweetpea and Honey grinned too. It sounded like their idea of utter bliss.

"Come along then. I've got the key," said Madame. "Saffron will be here soon."

The girls had never been inside the costume room before. Usually Madame or her assistant, Claudine, brought out rails of outfits before a big show. This was a very special treat. With a flick of the light switch, the rows of colourful costumes were brightly lit and the girls' eyes all danced around the room. There were rails of pastel tulle dresses, shelves full of ballet slippers and amazing hats and headdresses, and boys' costumes too, which none of the girls much liked to wear!

"Now," said Madame, "I thought we could arrange the room by ballet. For example, we could put all the *Cinderella* things over here and all the *Swan Lake* over there and so on."

The girls soon got lost in the task of arranging all the tulle skirts, satin tops and pretty flower and feather hair bands. They made a pile of all the garments that were in need of repair. Madame watched and was impressed by how well they worked as a team, with Poppy taking charge, Sweetpea being second in command and dear Honey doing as the other girls asked. Saffron soon arrived and showed them how to make

dainty repairs to the fragile costumes.
As they all sat merrily stitching and
chatting, Madame Angelwing told them
tales from the Russian ballet, which had
been passed on to her from her own
ballet teacher, Dame Petrina Karenina.
The girls, including Saffron, were
entranced.

When the costume room was all beautifully tidy, Madame told them to go through to the studio to try some new ballet steps, and before they knew it, their parents were peering in through the glass doors, ready to take them home.

"Aw, is it time to go home already?" said Poppy.

"It's been so much fun," smiled Honey. "Thank you, Madame Angelwing!"

"I can't wait till next Saturday," called Sweetpea as she gathered her things together.

And so the extra lessons went on. There were many magical moments for the three dedicated dancers. Sometimes Madame would allow them to do warm-up exercises to pop music. On other days she taught the girls some piano tunes, as she believed that understanding the music was the key to good timing. If there was time at the end of the lesson, she would read the girls a ballet

story. Sometimes *The Sleeping Beauty*,
sometimes *Coppelia*, and occasionally
The Nutcracker. The girls were living in
a ballet dream.

Chapter Three

"I love extra ballet so much!" said Poppy as she walked home with Mum and the twins after class one Saturday afternoon. "It's so much fun!"

"Well, I'm pleased to hear it, Poppy. Mind you, there were some things you did before these classes started that you seem to have forgotten about! Saffron and David called today to say that Twinkletoes is really missing you down at the stables. The twins hardly see you at the moment, and Grandpa was over for coffee earlier and he says that you never drop by after school any more," replied Mum. "He misses you and so do I. Not to mention Flossie and Posy. I've been feeding them both every day, and you know that's your job. And Posy's cage needs a clean really badly. Oh, and your room is a terrible mess, darling. You really must try to keep it tidy."

"Sorry, Mum," mumbled Poppy, "but it's really hard to do all that stuff with the ballet exam coming up. I've got normal ballet on Tuesdays, then extra ballet on Saturdays – sometimes a double lesson – and Madame Angelwing says we must do lots of practice in between lessons and learn as much about ballet as we can by reading all about it."

"Well, how about if I see to Twinkletoes and the other pets for the moment and help you keep your room tidy, but only if you promise me you'll start doing everything again after the exam. But I really would like you to go and see Grandpa this afternoon –

23

I don't care how much ballet stuff you've got on. Deal?"

"OK, Mum, deal," said Poppy.

Poppy had hardly thought about Grandpa at all during the last few weeks, which was very unusual as normally she saw him every day. She was living in a ballet bubble and forgetting everything else.

Just as she was getting ready to go over to Grandpa's house, the phone rang.

"Poppy!" called Mum. "It's Cousin Daisy for you!"

"Hi, Daisy!" said Poppy.

"Hello, Princess Poppy!" said Daisy. "Guess what? There's a pony club show next Saturday at Shellbay Park. I'm entering with Parsley and I was sure that you would want to do it too, so I've put your

name down for the beginner's class, with Twinkletoes! I think you've got a really good chance of winning a rosette, especially if we practise together this week."

"Oh, Daisy! Um, that sounds so cool but I have extra ballet lessons on Saturdays until the exams are over. I don't think I can do the show," said Poppy, feeling very disappointed indeed that she couldn't do both. She had wanted to be in a pony club show for as long as she could remember.

"No way," replied Daisy, sounding as disappointed as her younger cousin felt. "It's only one Saturday. Can't you miss the class just once?"

"Madame Angelwing says that riding is bad for ballerinas," replied Poppy. "Oh, but I so wish I could do both. It's not fair."

"Please, please say you'll do it!" begged Daisy. "It'll

be so much fun. Think about it and ring me back later today."

"OK, Daisy. I'll talk to you soon," agreed Poppy, bursting with excitement at the thought of riding in a show, but worrying about what she might miss if she skipped an extra class.

Poor Poppy felt very confused indeed. She wanted to be able to do both things but there simply wasn't enough time. She was going to have to choose.

While she lay on her bed wondering what to do, Grandpa was putting out milk

and biscuits specially for his little princess, but Poppy was so engrossed in her own problems that she completely forgot about her plan to visit him, and he was left all alone in his kitchen.

Eventually Poppy made a decision and went into the hall to ring her cousin.

"Hi, Daisy, it's Poppy. I'm really, really sorry but I've decided to go to ballet. I've just got to because the exam is so soon."

"Oh," said Daisy, who sounded very let down. "Never mind. It doesn't matter – have fun at ballet."

Poppy felt terrible – she could tell that

Daisy was upset, but what else was she to do?

"Oh no! Grandpa!" said Poppy, looking at the clock in the hall.

"Too late," said Mum crossly. "He's gone ballroom dancing at the Village Hall."

"Sorry!" said Poppy, feeling that she was letting everyone down.

Poppy and Honey carried on dancing non-stop, and Sweetpea did too. Madame made the classes such fun and they were improving all the time. Mimosa and Abigail were quite jealous of all the extra tuition their friends were receiving, but they'd missed their chance to join in now.

Poppy felt as if the extra lessons had made her a ballet star already. She put a *Swan Lake* poster from a ballet magazine up in her bedroom and went to sleep every night imagining she was dancing on the stage in a proper theatre, wearing a full white tutu and a fluffy feather headdress.

Chapter Four

One Monday morning about five weeks before the ballet exam, there was great excitement at school: Mimosa had brought in birthday party invitations.

"Have *you* got one?" squealed Abigail. "I have! I'm definitely going!"

Poppy couldn't wait to open her envelope – she adored birthday parties and had been looking forward to Mimosa's birthday for almost as long as Mimosa had!

Please come to my
Fairy Party
at the Hedgerows Hotel
on Saturday
12 - 2
fancy dress please,
fairy chants, fairy spells,
fairy dances and
fairy cakes!

Poppy's face fell.

"But I thought your birthday was on Sunday."

"It is, but my mum and dad have got a really big christening party in the hotel on Sunday, so I'm having the party on Saturday instead. We're going to pretend my birthday is a whole day earlier, which is cool 'cos I'll get my presents a whole day sooner!"

"Oh," replied Poppy. "But we've got a double extra ballet class on Saturday and it's at the same time."

"Please come," replied Mimosa quietly. "You're one of my best friends."

Poppy felt terrible. The last thing she wanted to do was upset Mimosa but she knew that Madame Angelwing would be cross if she skipped the class, plus she didn't want to miss out on any new steps.

"Can you come, Honey?" asked Mimosa nervously.

Honey looked very downcast. She had already decided not to go to Mimosa's fairy party – ballet was so important to her.

"I'm sorry, Mimi, I can't. Madame says it is very important that we don't miss classes. She says if we miss one, then we will lose the habit and I really, really want to get Honours in the exam. I'll make you a present, I promise!" said Honey.

Mimosa looked like she was about to

burst into tears. Two of her best friends were not going to come to her birthday party.

"Don't cry, Mimi," said Sweetpea sympathetically. "I'm going to come. I'm fed up with extra ballet. I want to do fun stuff on Saturdays, not be told off by Madame for not doing enough practice. I'm going to ask my mum if I can stop and just go on Tuesdays like you and Abi."

"I'm going to come too," said Abigail. "My piano lesson will be finished by twelve."

Mimosa was thrilled that Sweetpea and Abigail could come, but Poppy and Honey were both shocked that Sweetpea wanted to give up extra ballet.

"How can you even think about letting Madame down?" asked Honey.

"Easily. I don't want to be a famous ballerina. I like ballet, but I want time to do other stuff too," replied Sweetpea.

"Are you sure you can't come?" Mimosa asked Poppy. "You'd only miss the second part of your double class."

Just then, before Poppy had a chance to reply, the bell rang and the girls went back to their clasrooms.

After school Poppy told Mum about the clash between the fairy party and ballet and

how she didn't know what to do. She was desperate to go to Mimosa's party and didn't

want to upset her friend, but she didn't want
to let down Honey and Madame Angelwing
either.

"What would *you* like to do, darling?"
asked Mum.

"I don't know," confessed Poppy. "I want
to go to ballet *and* the party but I know I
can't do both. Whatever I do, I will hurt
someone's feelings."

"Well, you must do what is best for your
own feelings," said Mum. "I can't make the
decision for you."

At the end of the regular ballet class on
Tuesday, Madame called Poppy and Honey
aside.

"I will see you both on Saturday, yes? It
will just be you two girls. I am very sorry to
say that Sweetpea has decided to give up
extra ballet. It is quite understandable – it
was too much for her – but I know how
much you both enjoy it. You will continue
with the classes, won't you?" she asked.

Her voice was trembly and gentle and she was obviously quite hurt that Sweetpea had decided to stop the extra classes.

Poppy desperately wanted to tell her teacher that she couldn't come that Saturday because of the party, but she didn't want to upset her any more. She didn't have the courage to tell Madame how she really felt, so she stayed silent. Her decision had been made for her.

"Yes, Madame," said Poppy flatly. "See you on Saturday."

As she walked home after class, Poppy imagined what she might have worn to the party if she didn't have to go to ballet. She thought about all the fun fairy games and delicious fairy food that she was going to miss and how sad Mimosa was going to be. But then she thought about how upset

Madame would be if she called off extra ballet – and how disappointed Honey would be too.

Poppy saw Mimosa at school the next day.

"I'm so sorry, but I really won't be able to come to your party," she said sadly. "I just can't miss ballet."

Mimosa was very disappointed.

"I'll make you a present though, I promise," said Poppy, in an effort to cheer her friend up.

"Thank you," said Mimosa, feeling a little better. "I love presents! Do you and Honey want to come round after ballet to see all my birthday things?"

"Yes, please," smiled Poppy, and gave Mimosa a hug.

On the way back from ballet with Mum that Saturday, Poppy and Honey looked in the windows of the Hedgerows Hotel and

saw Mimosa's fairy party coming to an end.
All their friends were dressed in gorgeous
fairy outfits and were lining up to receive
their party bags from a pretty fairy
godmother. Poppy and Honey watched,
entranced, as all the fairies left with pink
fluffy bags in their hands.

"You two really missed out!" called
Abigail as she passed them on the drive with
several other girls dressed as fairies. "It was
the best party ever!"

"Yeah!" said Sweetpea. "It was brilliant —
much better than extra ballet. I'm so glad
I went!"

Honey and Poppy had made Mimosa a
jewellery casket out of a chocolate box, and
Poppy's mum had put some pretty coloured
beads inside it.

"Let's go in and give it to Mimosa,"
suggested Mum.

Mimosa was thrilled with the handmade
gift. "Thanks, girls!" she said. "I just wish you

could have been here. And I'm really sorry,
but all the cake and party bags are finished.
You can stay a while and help me open my
presents if you like."

"Yes, please," they chorused as they settled
down in front of Mimosa's pile of birthday
presents.

Mum had a coffee with Mrs Woodchester,
Mimosa's mum, while Poppy and Honey
helped Mimosa to write down every present
and who it was from, so she could write
thank-you notes.

"I'm sorry Poppy and Honey couldn't come," said Mrs Woodchester.

"Oh, so am I. Very sorry," said Mum. "These extra ballet classes are taking over our lives. I'm so proud of the girls for their commitment to ballet, but you know, they need to go to parties and other things too. I'm worried they're taking it a bit too seriously."

Mrs Woodchester nodded. "It's tricky. I mean, Mimosa wasn't too fussed at the beginning – she was more interested in earning extra pocket money on Saturday mornings. But now the exam is getting closer she would *love* to go to extra ballet classes, but Madame Angelwing won't have her. I admire the girls for going to the classes all this time. Mind you, Mimosa is always saying she hardly plays with Poppy and Honey outside of school any more because they're always doing ballet."

"I know how she feels," laughed Mum. "I

hardly see Poppy and she's my daughter!
Still, it will be over soon and everything will
go back to normal – or at least I hope it
will."

The next day was Sunday, and Grandpa,
Honey and Granny Bumble came over
for lunch. As Mum and Dad prepared a
delicious feast of roast chicken, vegetables
and gravy, Poppy and Honey chatted away
to Grandpa and Granny Bumble, telling
them all about what they'd been learning in
extra ballet. Then they played with the twins
– something Poppy hadn't done for
absolutely ages because she'd been so
wrapped up in ballet.

The girls even
dressed Angel up
as a ballerina and
tried to teach her
some simple steps.
Angel couldn't stop
giggling, and even

Archie tried to join in. Everyone laughed and clapped as the twins tried their best to copy their big sister and her friend.

"And now for the prima ballerinas," said Grandpa. "Let's see what's kept you too busy to visit your old grandpa any more!"

Poppy and Honey changed into their new outfits and put on a show. Everyone was so impressed with how they had progressed – their dedication had really paid off.

"Well, I'm sure you'll both do brilliantly in the exam," smiled Grandpa. "Well done for working so hard. Here's some pocket money to buy you each a ballet magazine."

"Thank you, Grandpa," said Poppy, beaming with pride. "I haven't bought this month's *Ballet Secrets* yet and it's got a free poster – I can put it up in my room along with my *Swan Lake* one."

"Thank you so much, Mr Mellow!" said Honey. "I'm going to get *Prima Ballerina* – it's got a really pretty necklace gift on the front."

Even Granny Bumble had to admit that her little granddaughter had come on in leaps and bounds. Perhaps Madame Angelwing was right: maybe Honey was good enough to become a professional ballerina one day.

"It's time you took a break from ballet, you lot. Lunch is ready!" called Dad from the dining room. "Come and sit down before it gets cold."

That night, as Poppy brushed her teeth and got ready for bed, she thought about what a lovely day she'd had – she hadn't had such a brilliant family day for ages and ages. In fact, not since she had started extra ballet classes. She realized how much she missed playing with the twins, chatting with Grandpa and listening to Dad's silly jokes. She had been concentrating so hard on ballet that it had completely taken over her life. She loved ballet – she was desperate to do well in the exam and to please Madame Angelwing – but she loved her family and friends more, and she really, really missed them.

Chapter Five

The next morning at school, Poppy was
supposed to be writing up her diary of
what had happened at the weekend but she
couldn't stop thinking about extra ballet
classes and the ballet exam. Should she carry
on with the classes until the exam or not?

"Poppy Cotton! Are you daydreaming
again?" said Miss Mallow. "What's wrong
with you at the moment? You look tired."

"Sorry, Miss Mallow," said Poppy. "I was
just thinking about the ballet exam."

"Hmmm, I see. Well, you're not in ballet

class now, so why don't you try thinking about your school work instead! There is more to life than ballet, you know, Poppy," said Miss Mallow, not unkindly.

"Yes, Miss Mallow, sorry," replied Poppy, thinking that her teacher was right, there definitely *was* more to life than ballet, although over the last few weeks it hadn't felt like it.

After morning break, which Honey spent in the gym practising ballet, there was a special lesson taken by Sally Meadowsweet from the Lavender Valley Garden Centre. She was showing the class how to knit, sew and embroider. Poppy loved craft and was very excited about learning some new skills, and by the end of the class she had successfully cast ten stitches onto her knitting needles and was busily making a scarf for Grandpa.

"I hope you all enjoyed today," said Sally at the end of the lesson. "If any of you are interested in learning more, I run a class in the Village Hall every week. Do come along and bring your families. Here's a flyer."

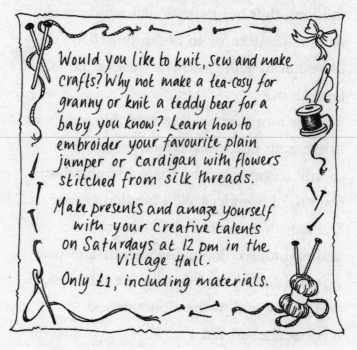

Would you like to knit, sew and make crafts? Why not make a tea-cosy for granny or knit a teddy bear for a baby you know? Learn how to embroider your favourite plain jumper or cardigan with flowers stitched from silk threads.

Make presents and amaze yourself with your creative talents on Saturdays at 12 pm in the Village Hall.
Only £1, including materials.

"I'd really like to come on Saturday," said Poppy. "I'll ask my mum if it's allowed."

"Great," replied Sally. "I hope to see you there – bring the twins too, if you like!"

That afternoon, after school, Poppy asked Mum if she could go to Sally's craft class.

"No, Poppy, I don't think you can. You just don't have enough time. You've got ballet until twelve this week and I'm already looking after your cat, your hamster and your pony and tidying your room. You'd have no time for lunch, or to see your friends and family. Maybe you can start craft lessons after the ballet exam: you'll have more free time then."

"But, Mum, I really want to do the craft lessons," replied Poppy. "And I've been thinking about ballet – I want to go back to just doing lessons on Tuesdays with all the other girls, if that's OK. I'm fed up with thinking about ballet all the time."

"Yes, darling, if it's what you want to do, then that's fine," said Mum, giving Poppy a big hug. "Well, I suppose I'd better speak to Madame Angelwing."

Grandpa babysat Poppy and the twins

while Mum made her way over to the
Lavender Lake School of Dance. She found
Madame in the studio.

"Ah, Lavender, what can I do for you?"
Madame asked.

"Well, Madame, I've just had a heart-
to-heart with Poppy and I'm afraid she's
decided to give up the extra ballet classes.
They are simply too much for her. She
doesn't have time for anything else. She is
neglecting her family, her friends and her
school work and she's exhausted," explained
Mum.

50

Madame looked very sad. "But the exams are not far off," she replied in a rather wobbly voice, "and she is progressing so well. Have I upset Poppy in any way? I know I can be strict, but my girls are my whole world."

"You have been amazingly sweet and patient with the girls, and Poppy has improved so much, I agree. She's just tired, that's all. I do hope you understand, and of course Poppy will be thrilled to come to normal Tuesday class and will continue to work hard for the exam," said Mum.

"I understand," said Madame. "I am very proud of all that we have achieved so far. Give Poppy my love. She's a great little princess."

Mum felt very upset about hurting Madame Angelwing's feelings, but she thought Poppy had come to the right decision and she very much hoped that things would get back to normal again.

Only Honey was left going to extra ballet classes. She was still as keen as ever to get Honours in the exam and she dreamed about going to proper ballet school one day. Although she was sad that Poppy had stopped the extra classes, it was wonderful to have one-on-one tuition with her beloved ballet teacher – it made her even more determined to work hard and to please Madame.

Madame was very sweet to both Sweetpea and Poppy at Tuesday ballet lessons, but she was really thrilled with Honey for being so very dedicated, and she even started teaching her on Thursdays after school as well as on Saturdays and Tuesdays.

Granny Bumble was worried about Honey and tried to talk to her about taking a break and not tiring herself out, but Honey wouldn't listen.

"Granny, please don't stop me from doing

extra ballet. I really, really want to get Honours in the exam and Madame says I will if I keep working hard and practising. Please don't make me give up 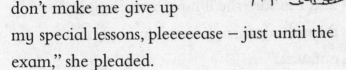 my special lessons, pleeeeease – just until the exam," she pleaded.

"All right, sweetheart," agreed Granny Bumble reluctantly. "But promise me you won't overdo it – you look tired."

On Saturday, after lunch, Poppy made her way round to Honeypot Cottage, hoping to see Honey.

"Hi, Poppy," called Granny Bumble from the Bakehouse. "I'm afraid Honey isn't back from ballet yet, love. A double lesson again today, what with the exams coming up and whatnot."

"Oh!" said Poppy, feeling very disappointed that her friend wasn't there. "Well, can you tell her that I was looking for her, please? She can come over to play whenever she likes. We haven't played in the tree house together for ages."

"I miss her too, Poppy," said Granny Bumble. "But the ballet exam is very soon and I'm sure she'll have some more time for us both then. I certainly hope so anyway!"

When Poppy got home, she was quite sad. "Mum, I really miss Honey. I can sort of see how you and Grandpa felt when I was doing a lot of ballet," she said.

"Well, cheer up, darling. My old friend from school, Felicity Darling, called here earlier. She's sending her daughter, Blossom, to ballet classes at Lavender Lake, as the ballet school at Strawberry Corner is closing down. She thought it would be nice if Blossom got together with you so

54

that she knows someone when she starts ballet. I've asked them both over on Monday after school."

"That sounds great – I can show her my tree house and we can play dress-up!" said Poppy, feeling a bit brighter.

On Monday afternoon Blossom came to play as Mum had promised. Poppy looked out of the window as the Darlings' car drew up. Blossom was very pretty and dainty and

she had a cute baby sister called Freya, who
was about Archie and Angel's age.

As soon as the Darlings came in, the older
girls went to play while the mums chatted
and played with the babies.

Poppy thought Blossom was really nice,
and very good at ballet – as far as Poppy
could tell when they compared steps in the

play room.

"I think Madame Angelwing will love you!" said Poppy encouragingly, remembering how the ballet teacher had reacted when Honey started ballet.

Blossom smiled gratefully. She was quite shy and nervous about joining a new ballet class so near to the exam, so it felt good to have Poppy as a friend.

Over a delicious tea of cottage pie, followed by apple sponge pudding, Poppy and Blossom chatted away happily. Soon it was time for Blossom and her family to leave.

"See you at ballet," called Poppy as Blossom waved goodbye through the car window. "Byeee!"

"Well done, Poppy," said Mum as they turned to go back into the house. "You've really helped Blossom feel welcome in your ballet class. What a kind princess you are!"

Chapter Six

Poppy and Honey saw very little of each other in the weeks leading up to the exam. On Tuesdays at normal ballet class, Honey seemed very distant from her friends, as she had been taught lots of different steps. She would stand at the barre doing her own thing, with Madame Angelwing occasionally calling out: "Bravo, Honey!" Poppy wasn't jealous of Honey; she was just worried about her. Honey could think of nothing but ballet and she was looking very tired.

"You know what, Mum," said Poppy at

tea time after ballet one day, "I think Honey will be too tired to take the ballet exam. She is doing so much practice."

Mum looked concerned. "Dear little Honey – it sounds like she's really overdoing it."

"And, Mum," continued Poppy, "Honey never plays fairy princesses at break any more. And she doesn't play on the swings. She's always in the gym hall, practising ballet. And Miss Mallow is getting quite worried and cross because Honey doesn't do such neat work any more and she's always sleepy."

"Oh, dear! That is a worry. I think I'd better have a chat with Granny Bumble later," replied Mum. "You are being a good friend to Honey, you know."

After supper Mum left Dad in charge of

Poppy and the twins and popped out to see Granny Bumble. She rang the bell at Honeypot Cottage and Granny Bumble opened the door.

"Come in, Lavender, dear. How nice to see you. And what can I do for you?"

"Well, I wanted to talk to you about Honey, actually," said Mum. "Is she around?"

"She's just gone up to bed. She's absolutely shattered – nearly fell asleep over supper!" sighed Granny Bumble. "I hope she's not done anything wrong."

"Oh no, nothing like that," smiled Mum. "I'm just worried about her."

"Why don't you take a seat? I'll make some tea, and you can tell me all about it," said Granny Bumble kindly.

A couple of minutes later she came through to her cosy sitting room with a pot of scented tea and a tray of freshly baked cherry muffins. Mum told her what Poppy had said.

"I'm quite worried myself," explained Granny Bumble, "and I've tried to talk to her about taking things a bit easier and not doing just ballet, but Honey just says I'm trying to spoil her chances if I suggest she has a break. If it's affecting her school work and Poppy has noticed that she's tired out and doing ballet at break instead of playing, then I think I have to do something."

"Well, I think there's only one solution," said Mum. "You'll have to explain things to Madame Angelwing and ask her to tell Honey that there's no need for her to have extra lessons any more. That way, Honey won't blame you."

"Yes, but you know what Eloise Angelwing is like. Very touchy. Highly strung. She'll take it badly as Honey is the last one of the girls left going to the extra classes. I'm being a coward, aren't I?" replied Granny Bumble.

"It is difficult," said Mum sympathetically, "but it's one of those jobs that just has to be done."

"You're right. I'll invite Eloise over to the teashop for a cup of tea and a scone tomorrow and I'll talk things through with her," decided Granny Bumble.

"Great!" said Mum. "Poppy and Honey need to go back to hanging out together, playing *and* taking care of poor old

Twinkletoes. She'll thank you in the end, you know."

The next morning Granny Bumble waited nervously in Bumble Bees Teashop. She saw Madame Angelwing approach and pulled out two chairs. Madame took a seat and Granny Bumble poured a cup of peppermint tea and placed a toasted teacake on a plate. She sighed as she began to explain everything to the ballet teacher, who sat quietly but looked more and more upset as Granny Bumble spoke.

"Of course I understand that Honey must have a break, Mrs Bumble. I wish someone had told me that I was getting too carried away. Poor lamb! She is so special to me – as are all the girls, but Honey in particular."

"Honey adores you and so do the other girls, Madame, but they're only little and they get tired very easily."

Madame understood the situation and, between them, she and Granny Bumble decided that the best thing would be for Honey to give up the Thursday classes and take it easy with her practice, but to continue with the Tuesday and Saturday lessons. Madame Angelwing very sweetly agreed that she would speak to Honey as Granny Bumble knew that Honey would only listen to her ballet teacher.

"I'll tell Honey at the next lesson," she promised.

"Thank you so much, Eloise," said Granny Bumble gratefully.

When Honey turned up at the Lavender Lake School of Dance on Thursday,

Madame Angelwing was waiting outside
for her.

"I thought we'd just go for a walk today,
Honey dear. Don't get changed into your
ballet things."

Honey was surprised. She had perfected
a pirouette routine that she was eager to
show Madame, but she did as she was told.
They strolled along the River Swan.

"Honey, you have a very fine talent for ballet," began Madame. "You are as good if not better than I was at your age. You are going to do very well in the ballet exam, I know you are. In fact you are more than ready for it. But you know, in the world of ballet we have something called burn-out. What it refers to is a kind of exhaustion or tiredness where we have worked so hard that we are in danger of collapse. Now, the last thing I want is for you get that tired, sweetheart. So I suggest we don't do any more extra classes on Thursdays. It will only do you harm if you do too much. You must come to normal class on Tuesdays and your special Saturday class. You must rest well and eat lots of fresh fruit, vegetables and grains. We can do some fun ballet things together after the exam."

Honey felt tears well up in her eyes and she looked away. She didn't really understand what Madame meant except that her special Thursday classes were going to stop. Madame thought she might cry too. She was so attached to Honey, who was the closest thing to a granddaughter she would ever have.

"Oh, Honey, please don't be upset. It is for the best, I promise. Let's go to the teashop now, dear," said Madame, taking Honey's fragile little hand in her own.

But Honey broke away, tears streaming down her face, and ran to find her granny.

Chapter Seven

When Honey didn't come to school on
Friday, Poppy was worried and decided
to go and see her friend later that day.

"I'm sorry, Poppy," said Granny Bumble,
"but Honey's not well. She's very tired and
has a sore throat and the sniffles, so she's
in bed."

"Oh," replied Poppy, disappointed that she
couldn't see her friend. "Tell her I hope she
gets well soon."

"I will do. You have a good weekend,"
said Granny Bumble.

By Tuesday, with only two weeks until the
exam, Honey was feeling much better. As
she arrived at the dance studio, she saw
Poppy talking to a small pretty blonde girl.

"Hi, Honey!" called Poppy. "How are
you? This is Blossom. She's doing her exam
with us because her dance school has closed
down. She's really good at ballet, just
like you!"

Blossom blushed and Honey smiled shyly
at her. She thought that Blossom looked like
a true ballerina. She had a beautiful blonde
bun at the back of her head and was

wearing a gorgeous white net ballet skirt over a white leotard and a soft shell-pink cotton crossover cardigan.

Just then, Mimosa, Sweetpea and Abigail rushed over to say hi. They had been worried about Honey and were glad that she was well enough to come to class again. And they wanted to know why she was no longer taking extra classes on Thursdays.

"What happened, Honey? Did you want to stop the lessons?" asked Mimosa.

"No, it wasn't my idea. I just don't get it," said Honey sadly, making her way towards the barre.

"Didn't you ask Madame why?" queried Sweetpea.

But before Honey had a chance to reply, Madame came sweeping into the class in one of her pretty, long, floaty pink dresses, with her pink pashmina around her shoulders. She smiled at Honey and then asked everyone to stand in first position.

"I would like to introduce you to a new pupil today, girls," said Madame, beckoning Blossom to come forward. "This is Blossom Darling, from Strawberry Corner. She has been taught by my dear friend Lavinia-Jane Forbes, of the Forbes Dance Academy. Unfortunately Lavinia has had to retire due to ill health. Dear Lavinia, we were in the *corps de ballet* together many years ago . . ."

When Madame emerged from the other end of her ballet story, poor Blossom was looking very pink-cheeked, staring out at a sea of curious faces.

As the lesson commenced, it soon became clear that Blossom was quite advanced compared to most of the girls. However, because of Honey's natural ability and all the extra tuition she had received, she was easily a match for her. Madame was very impressed by her new pupil.

"Dear child. Lavinia said you had a gift, but what a gift it is, indeed!" she exclaimed.

Honey felt herself choke with jealousy. *Don't be silly!* she thought. *Madame has said things like that to you a hundred times. Blossom is a lovely dancer — so what?*

But Honey was feeling very fragile indeed. She still didn't see why she'd had to stop her Thursday lessons, and now Madame appeared to have a new favourite – Blossom Darling.

"Now, Blossom, how is your *petit jeté*?" asked Madame. "The examiners from the Royal Academy set great store by the *petit jeté*. Let me see, Blossom dear."

Blossom blushed again. "I'm sorry, Madame, I have never been shown that step. Madame Forbes has been poorly for a few weeks. She said she was going to teach it to us, but she wasn't well enough."

"I see," said Madame Angelwing. "That is a worry. Oh, it is a worry indeed! I'll tell you what, Blossom: I could give you some extra lessons this Thursday and next and teach you the steps you've missed out on. I'll ask your mother when she comes to pick you up."

"Thank you, Madame Angelwing," replied Blossom sweetly.

Honey saw a flash of green jealousy before her eyes, followed by a cloud of red anger. *She* was Madame's special pupil. So this was why Madame had stopped her Thursday classes –

so that she could give Blossom all her
attention! It all became clear to Honey.
Madame had a new favourite pupil.

It was unlike Honey to feel so jealous
and cross. And much as she thought
Blossom was probably a very nice girl, she
couldn't help blaming her for taking
Madame away from her.

Poppy could see that Honey was feeling
very sad indeed. As they walked back to the
teashop together after class, she tried to find
out what was wrong.

"What's the matter, Honey?"

"Madame doesn't like me any more. Blossom is her new best girl and it's not fair. What have I done wrong?" asked Honey. "I just don't understand."

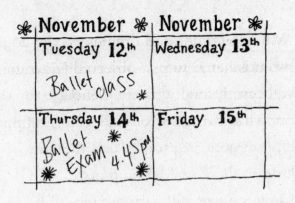

❋ November ❋	❋ November ❋
Tuesday 12th	Wednesday 13th
Ballet class ❋	
Thursday 14th	Friday 15th
Ballet ❋ Exam ❋ 4.45pm	

Chapter Eight

Over the next two weeks, the Lavender Lake girls became more and more jealous of Blossom Darling. She danced well, looked lovely, and Madame was giving her lots of personal attention.

With only two days to go before the exam, the girls went to the dance school for their Tuesday class. As instructed by Madame, they had all brought along their new outfits for the exam in their ballet cases, which were to be left in the changing rooms until Thursday.

"We don't want any dramas on the day about tights and tutus!" observed Madame. "I've been through this often enough to know what can go wrong. Place everything neatly on your peg today, and then on Thursday there will be no tears."

Madame was still very anxious that Blossom should learn all the steps she had missed. She was confident that all her girls knew them well enough, so at snack time Blossom stayed in the studio to perfect her *demi-pliés*.

"Why's she getting special treatment?" asked Sweetpea as the other girls tucked into their snacks. "I know that we got extra help, but that's because we've been here for ages. Blossom only turned up a couple of weeks ago. Teacher's pet already, or what?"

"Yeah, I know," replied Mimosa. "She's definitely Madame's favourite."

No one expected Honey to join in as she never usually had a bad word to say about anybody, but this was different.

"It's like she's extra-special — and it's all because of her that my Thursday lessons have stopped," she moaned. "It's not fair." Somehow Honey's comments made everyone turn against Blossom even more, and all the girls except Poppy started being mean about her. Honey wasn't behaving at all like herself at the moment, Poppy thought. Normally she was very easy to get along with, but recently she didn't want to do anything. Even ballet, which used to be her favourite thing in the whole world, was making her miserable. Poppy just didn't know what to do.

When they went back into the studio for the second half of their lesson, they saw that Blossom was doing beautifully with her *demi-pliés* and they all felt even more jealous of her.

"Now please leave your outfits for the exam in the changing room. And, girls, remember to sleep well before the exam, and

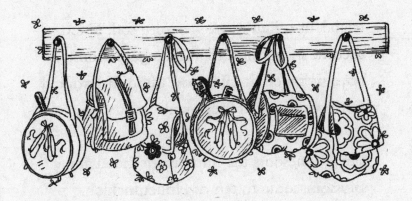

eat lots of fruit and vegetables, and a little
pasta," said Madame Angelwing at the end
of the lesson.

"Yes, Madame," chorused the girls. "See
you on Thursday."

When Poppy's mum picked up Poppy and
Honey that evening, she mentioned to
Poppy that she'd invited Blossom and her
mum over for tea the next day. Although
Poppy really liked Blossom, she wished that
Mum hadn't said anything in front of
Honey: when she looked over at her best
friend, she could see that Honey was upset
and cross about Blossom. Little by little,
Poppy felt that she was losing her best

friend, and that made her very sad. They used to spend all their time together and have so much fun. The last thing she wanted to do was make Honey sad.

On Wednesday, the day before the exam, Blossom came to tea at Honeysuckle Cottage. As usual, Blossom and Poppy went off to play, while Mrs Darling and Mum chatted away in the kitchen. But when Poppy went to get some milk for her and Blossom, she overheard Mrs Darling saying something about Blossom.

"It is so kind, what Madame Angelwing is doing for Blossom. But do you know why she is helping her so much? It's because Blossom's previous teacher, Lavinia-Jane Forbes, asked her to make sure Blossom was ready for the exam as a personal favour. Lavinia had very high hopes for Blossom. But between you and me, Blossom is terribly embarrassed that she is getting special treatment. She hates being the centre of attention and she's worried that the other girls won't like her because of it. Of course, Poppy is being very sweet to her and making her feel welcome."

"Oh dear, poor Blossom," sympathized Mum, suspecting that the other girls were jealous of her already.

Poppy felt very bad for her new

friend – she knew that the other girls were
jealous of her. She decided to tell Honey and
the others what she'd overheard. She hoped
they would understand and would stop
being mean to Blossom.

The two girls had a lovely spaghetti tea
together and talked about the ballet exam.
Then they had a final practice in Poppy's
sitting room before it was time for Blossom
to go home.

"Sleep well," said Poppy as Blossom
climbed into her car. "Ballet dreams!"

The next day at school Poppy had that
funny butterfly feeling in her tummy all day

because of the exam, and because she was worried about Blossom. At break she tried to tell the girls why Madame Angelwing was being so nice to Blossom, but they wouldn't listen.

"Poppy, she's being given special treatment and it's not fair on Honey. Stop sticking up for her and think about your best friend for a change," said Mimosa.

Honey smiled shyly. She was glad that most of her friends understood how hurt she was feeling, even if her best friend didn't.

Everyone arrived promptly for the exam at the Lavender Lake School of Dance and changed into comfy T-shirts and joggers for their warm-up routine.

"Mimosa, what took you so long in the changing room?" asked Madame Angelwing as Mimosa came out five minutes after the other girls. "You know how important it is to warm up before ballet. Today is an important day and we do not have much time."

"Sorry, Madame, I just wanted to get a glass of water. I was thirsty," replied Mimosa as she joined in with the stretches and bends that the other girls were doing.

After their gentle warm-up Madame sent the girls off to the changing room to get ready for the exam.

"Only twenty minutes until the examiner arrives!" said Madame. "Good luck, girls!"

"I'm so nervous," exclaimed Abigail as she pulled on her tights. "We've got the strictest examiner in the country!"

"I'm not going to remember a single step!" worried Sweetpea. "I wish I had carried on with the special classes!"

"You'll be fine," said Honey reassuringly.

"Oh no! My ballet clothes – they've gone!" cried Blossom as she reached her peg.

Chapter Nine

Poppy guessed exactly what had happened
– her friends had hidden Blossom's new
ballet stuff. She was too confused to know
what to do. She really liked Blossom but she
didn't want Honey, her best friend in the
whole world, to get into trouble. There was
no way that Blossom would be allowed to
sit a Royal Academy exam in a pair of
navy-blue jogging trousers.

Madame Angelwing, Blossom and Poppy
hunted high and low for the missing outfit
but with no luck.

"This has never happened before!" shrieked Madame in total panic. "We've been short of a pair of tights or a head band, yes, but a whole outfit? Never! We must find it."

There were only ten minutes left until the first exam. All the other girls were sitting at the mirrors in the dressing room finishing their hair.

"We can't tell the truth now," whispered Mimosa to Honey. "We'll just have to put the clothes back after the exam."

Honey nodded, although she was already feeling terrible about what they'd done to Blossom.

Madame frantically called Blossom's mum to ask her to bring a new outfit but there was no reply on Mrs Darling's phone.

"Blossom can wear one of my old outfits,"

suggested Poppy. "I'll run home for it!"

"Nonsense, Poppy dear. That is very kind, but there isn't enough time for that," said Madame. "We'll find Blossom's outfit if we all search. Girls, look all round the changing room and in the studio and anywhere else you can think of."

Mimosa panicked. She hadn't thought there would be time for a search party. What if someone found the clothes in her locker? She was going to be in the biggest trouble! Everyone was scurrying around looking in cupboards and under chairs, when Blossom had an idea.

"Madame Angelwing,

maybe it got into someone else's locker by mistake."

"Oh, yes. Everyone, check your lockers now," commanded Madame.

Just as everyone went towards their lockers, and as Mimosa started to breathe more quickly in her panic, the doorbell rang. Madame Angelwing let out a yelp.

"Lady Margery from the Academy! My girls! Get to the barre and limber! Limber as gracefully as you can!"

Mimosa let out a sigh of relief but poor Blossom burst into floods of tears.

"What will I wear?" she wailed, looking down at her scruffy jogging trousers.

"Oh . . . um! I know what!" said Madame. "Take this key and help yourself to something from the costume room. Anything that fits, dear. And then come back to the studio as quickly as you can!"

Honey, Sweetpea and Mimosa were beginning to feel really bad about what they had done. Maybe they should give back the outfit, but they couldn't think how and now there was no time. But when they heard Madame Angelwing's suggestion about the costume room, they felt cross with Blossom all over again.

"Huh! She will look better than all of us. It's so unfair. How does she always luck out?" whispered Sweetpea to the other two.

"I know!" agreed Mimosa.

While Poppy was glad that Blossom was going to be able to take the exam after all, she felt very alone because ballet had come between her and her friends. She didn't know what to do.

Blossom let herself into the costume room and chose a pale pink vintage tutu that Madame had brought from the Paris ballet house. It was a dress that Honey and Sweetpea had helped Saffron to repair several weeks before. Little did Blossom know that she had picked the very dress that

was going to make the girls even more
jealous and annoyed with her.

Honey was upset that Blossom had
triumphed again and that their horrible
prank had gone wrong; now the new girl
had even more of Madame Angelwing's
sympathy *and* she looked wonderful.
However, Honey tried really hard to focus
on performing well in her exam.

Lady Margery called all the girls
individually into the small private studio

where Madame usually did her paperwork. Poppy went first. She tried very hard to remember everything Madame had told her. Straight back, shoulders back, smile and be graceful. She got through the steps well, and then, when it came to the free dance, she danced the part of *Cinderella* beautifully.

"That's all," said Lady Margery as she ticked boxes on a page in front of her. "You may go."

Poppy curtsied and danced out of the room, delighted that she had survived the exam. As far as she knew, she hadn't messed it up.

Next in was Mimosa, followed by Abigail. Then it was Honey's turn. She was feeling very hot and sick, but she knew she had to do it. Ballet was her thing. She *must* succeed. When she was in the studio, she forgot about all her jealousies and problems and danced as though her life depended on it. For the free dance she performed the Sugarplum

Fairy from *The Nutcracker*, and judging by
the smile on Lady Margery's face, she was
very impressed.

When all the girls from the Lavender
Lake School of Dance had performed, it
was time for Blossom to go in. She floated
into the studio like a real fairy in her
gorgeous tutu.

"Good luck!" called Poppy, ignoring
the scowls of her other friends.

Blossom was very quiet when she
came out.

"How did it go?" whispered Poppy.

"Pretty good, I think," replied Blossom, grateful that at least someone was being kind to her, but keen not to show off.

By the time Blossom got to the changing room, her own outfit was back on her peg, as if by magic.

Poor Blossom knew that the other girls had hidden her stuff and she was very upset. As she got dressed, she brushed a tear from her cheek and wished more than anything that the girls would just be nice to her.

Chapter Ten

Next Tuesday at ballet Sweetpea, Mimosa, Honey and Abigail were still feeling grumpy that their plan had backfired. When they walked into the dance studio, along with Poppy and Blossom, they found Madame looking very serious indeed.

"I have here a poem about myself, girls, which was sent to me by post," said Madame as she put on her spectacles. She started to read it aloud.

> A terrible thing:
> Poor Madame Angelwing,
> Her knicker elastic went **PING !**
> She had to tie them with string,
> Then she did the Highland fling.
> She was tripped up by the string,
> So her arm was put in a sling !
> What a terrible thing,
> For poor Madame Angelwing !

Some of the girls began to giggle, which made Madame even crosser.

"Well, is anyone going to admit to sending this to me? I am very hurt by this – it is not a funny joke."

There was silence in the studio.

"As it happens, the postmark on the envelope is Strawberry Corner. And we only have one pupil from Strawberry Corner here, don't we?" said Madame crisply. "Do you know anything about this, Blossom?"

Blossom's face was bright red. "No, Madame. I didn't write that, or send it," she protested.

"Now, Blossom, I hope you are telling the truth. It is bad enough to play such a prank, but to deny it is worse still."

"Somebody help me, please!" begged Blossom, starting to sob. "I didn't do it! Why is everyone except Poppy so mean to me?"

Poppy looked at Honey. She desperately wanted to help sort everything out but she didn't want to get Honey into trouble. Honey saw the look of frustration on her best friend's face and could bear it no longer. She stood up with her cheeks burning.

"Madame, it is my fault. I wanted to get at Blossom for taking over my special lessons on Thursdays. And it was my fault that her ballet outfit disappeared on the day of the exam. I am truly sorry. I just didn't understand why you stopped my lessons. I thought it was so that you could give lessons to Blossom instead."

Sweetpea, Mimosa and Abigail stood up too.

"It's not all Honey's fault. We were annoyed with Blossom too. Poor Honey lost her Thursday lessons because of her. We've been sticking up for Honey 'cos she's been really sad and she's our friend," explained Sweetpea truthfully.

"I'm just as bad," confessed Mimosa. "I asked my dad to post the poem in Strawberry Corner. I told him it was a thank-you card to you."

Madame looked shocked, confused and then furious. "I am terribly disappointed in you, girls. You are supposed to be young ladies. This is the first time in my whole career that such a thing has happened. I am lost for words."

She paced around the studio with her head in her hands while all the girls remained silent. Those who had been involved in the pranks now felt very sorry indeed. Their meanness seemed even more dreadful now that it was out in the open.

"Sweetpea, Abigail, Mimosa and Honey, you must apologize to Blossom most sincerely," said Madame Angelwing, after what felt like an age. "She did not deserve this treatment. You have been very cruel."

The girls each went to Blossom and said how sorry they were. They really meant it too. And slowly Madame softened and looked tenderly at Honey, who was shaking with nerves.

"Ah, Honey, there is much you have not understood, dear child. I was asked to stop giving you extra lessons by those who care deeply for you. They thought you were too

tired and that your school work and your
health were suffering. And when this was
brought to my attention, I was truly worried
that you might suffer from burn-out. And
as for Blossom, she is a dear child, but
the reason she has had extra help is out
of respect to my friend Lavinia, who
helped me to establish my school of dance
when I first moved here from Paris many
years ago."

Blossom looked at Honey and Honey
looked back, with tears of shame spilling
down her cheeks. The dance teacher felt a
mixture of strong emotions. She saw all of
a sudden that these were children before her,

not grown-up ballerinas, and she began to feel very sorry for her behaviour.

"This misunderstanding is my fault too!" she said. "Grown-ups! What fools we are, not thinking how you might feel at times. But, girls, my girls, I do not expect this sort of bad behaviour from you. Ballet should be about friendship, not fighting!"

"We are truly sorry, Madame!" said all the girls, including Honey, who was sorriest of all.

"Well," began Madame Angelwing as she rearranged her pink pashmina, "I think it's time for ballet to be fun again! Let me take you all to the city to see *Swan Lake* this weekend. I was going to take you when the results came through, but who cares about the results, if we can't be friends?"

"Hurrah!" cried the girls. "Thank you, Madame!"

That Saturday, Madame Angelwing took

Poppy, Mimosa, Honey, Sweetpea, Blossom and Abigail to the matinée performance of *Swan Lake*. They had all dressed up in special outfits for their treat, and on the way up to the City on the train they admired one another's gorgeous clothes.

Honey thought that Blossom looked especially pretty in a lilac tulle dress, with matching flowers in her hair and a cosy lilac velvet coat, as the autumn winds were starting to bite.

"You look lovely, Blossom," said Honey sweetly.

"Thank you! So do you," replied Blossom politely, admiring Honey's golden yellow party dress, with matching cape.

When they arrived at the theatre, Madame carefully handed out the tickets to the girls. Honey sat between Poppy and Blossom. She smiled shyly, desperately hoping that one day Blossom would forgive her for being so mean, and she was pleased when Blossom smiled back.

The curtains swished apart and the performance began. The girls were immediately mesmerized by the sad and beautiful story of Princess Odette, who along with the other girls had been turned into a swan by an evil sorcerer. Honey found the story a little confusing and looked to Blossom for help.

"That is Odile, the nasty girl who looks exactly like Odette!" whispered Blossom

kindly. "Prince Siegfried is getting them mixed up."

"Oh, thanks," whispered Honey. "I kind of know the story but it is really complicated!"

Blossom smiled and offered Honey a fruit sweet.

"Thanks, Blossom," said Honey as she settled down to watch the rest of the performance.

When the ballet was over, they made their way back to the railway station and caught the train home. When they arrived back in Honeypot Hill, Honey turned to Blossom.

"I'm sorry I've been more like Odile than Odette lately. I promise I will never be mean again."

"I don't blame you, Honey. I should never have joined a new ballet school so near to exam time. I hope we can be friends."

"Of course we can!" said Honey, smiling broadly.

Poppy hugged Honey. "I knew you two were going to get along! But don't leave me out by being ballet bores, will you?"

They all laughed.

Everyone enjoyed Tuesday ballet classes over the next few weeks, as well as all their other hobbies and outings. One Tuesday they arrived to find Madame in a state of great excitement. The exam results had arrived from the Royal Academy. The girls all held hands as Madame read them out.

"Honey Bumble and Blossom Darling have Honours! Congratulations, girls. Bravo! And I am proud to announce that every other girl at Lavender Lake has Highly Commended, which is a brilliant result. I am overjoyed. Delighted."

The girls were all thrilled with their results and felt very grateful to Madame for preparing them so well for the exam.

"Well done, Poppy!" said Mum on the way home after ballet. "Are you happy, darling?"

"Yeah, but mainly because Honey and Blossom are friends and ballet is fun again."

Mum smiled. She was very proud of her little princess.

At break time the next Monday all the ballet girls got together and decided that they wanted to do something nice to say thank you to Madame Angelwing for being such a good teacher and for taking them to the ballet – and to say sorry for all the trouble they had caused.

"I know what!" said Poppy. "Let's surprise her by acting out a scene from *Swan Lake* for her at ballet tomorrow. We can wear the costumes we mended. I know where she keeps the key to the costume room!"

"Cool idea!" agreed the girls.

"But we must let Blossom know," said Honey thoughtfully, thinking of their friend, who was at a different school.

All the girls, including Blossom, met at Poppy's house after school to practise their routine. The next day they sneaked into the dance school straight after school, went to the costume room, put on their pretty swan outfits and crept into the studio to wait for Madame to arrive.

As soon as they heard her high heels clip-clopping along the corridor, Poppy started the *Swan Lake* music, and they began their performance as Madame walked through the door. She was absolutely enchanted.

"My girls! My little ballerinas! My swans – all Odettes! Not an Odile amongst you!" she cried.

The girls giggled and hugged Madame. She may have been strict, she may have been difficult to please, but she had a heart of gold and wanted the very best for her girls.

When all the mums came to pick up their daughters, Madame searched for Poppy's mum.

"I just wanted to say something,

Lavender. Poppy may not have got Honours in the ballet exam, but over the last few weeks her kindness has been of Honours standard as far as I am concerned."

Mum was overflowing with pride.

"Mum, want to know a secret?" asked Poppy that night. "I still have ballet dreams, you know!"

"And because you are so kind and thoughtful, I believe all your dreams will come true one day, my beautiful ballet princess!" smiled Mum.

"I think I'll just go and see Grandpa!" said Poppy, dancing down the garden like Princess Odette.

Turn over to read an extract from
the next Princess Poppy book,
Pop Star Princess . . .

You're a star...

competition coming soon in Camomile Cove ✕ ✕ ✕

Chapter One

Poppy and Honey were so excited. Along with Poppy's older cousin, Daisy, and her two friends, Lily and Rose, they were the Beach Babes. In just two weeks' time they were going to be taking part in the local heats of the *You're a Star!* talent contest, which were being filmed in Camomile Cove.

Poppy and Honey had been backing singers for Daisy's band ever since the Smuggler's Cove High School Battle of the Bands the summer before and they couldn't wait to perform with them again.

"It will be so cool if we win," said Poppy breathlessly. "I can't wait."

"But won't there be loads of other really good bands taking part?" asked Honey, already feeling a bit nervous about the whole thing. "Do you think we have a *real* chance of winning?"

"I think we will definitely be the best," replied Poppy confidently. "Saffron is going to make our stage outfits, Madame Angelwing's assistant, Claudine, is going to teach us a brilliant dance routine, and I know that Daisy, Lily and Rose are working on a really cool new song."

"Ooooh, how exciting!" replied Honey. "I love dancing!"

"Me too," giggled Poppy, "and it's mainly you and me doing the dancing because the others will be playing their instruments. I bet none of the other bands will have a proper dance routine. I've made a plan with Daisy that we'll meet her, Lily and Rose at the Lavender Lake School of Dance on Saturday at ten o'clock. They're going to play us the song and Claudine is going to start teaching us our dance."

"What's the new song like?" asked Honey.

"Ummm, I don't actually know yet because they're still writing it," explained Poppy. "Daisy said that they're meeting in her summer house every day after school to work on the words and the music."

"I wish I had a cool cousin like you do," sighed Honey, who thought her life might be rather dull without the connections of her beloved best friend.

"Daisy practically *is* your cousin, Honey!" laughed Poppy. "You see her just as much as I do."

On Saturday morning, Poppy and Honey set off to meet Daisy and her friends. They were desperate to hear the new song and so excited to be involved.

When they arrived at the dance studio, Daisy, Lily and Rose were already there. Poppy hugged her cousin and said 'Hi' to the other two girls, and Honey shyly followed suit.

"Is the song finished?" asked Poppy. "Can we hear it?"

"Hang on a minute," laughed Daisy. "We've only just got here. We need to set everything up first."

"OK," replied Poppy, "but can you at least tell me what the song's called?"

"It's called *Chocolate Sundae Girls*. It was inspired by our favourite treat at the Lighthouse Café! And, even better," Daisy continued, "the owners of the café, Fleur and Harvey, have said that if we win the competition, we'll all get free chocolate sundaes for the rest of the year!"

Poppy thought that the Lighthouse Café was the coolest place on earth and she knew that their chocolate sundaes were heavenly. "Wow!" she said. "Deeelicious!"

Just then Claudine came out of the staff room, ready to get to work, and Daisy pressed PLAY on the CD player. The Beach Babes' new song filled the room and all the girls, including Claudine, couldn't help dancing and humming along to its catchy pop tune and brilliant words:

> Sittin' at the window table
> Waitin' for our dreams to come,
> We don't have designer labels,
> We are nobodies to some.
>
> Give our order to the girl,
> She brings a treat for us to share,
> Chocolate sauce for us to swirl,
> Fluffy ice cream everywhere.

Daisy, Lily and Rose were thrilled that everybody liked their song – they'd put so much hard work into it. But there was still lots to do before the talent contest.

"Let's get going with the dance routine for Poppy and Honey!" urged Daisy. "Claudine, what do you think we should do?"

"I have this idea that we should base it around street café life. What do you think?" she asked as she showed the girls a scenario she had in mind, where the younger girls started singing while sitting at chairs at a round table in the middle of the stage. Gradually they would get up and start dancing and singing around the table, picking up their tambourines and shaking them from time to time.

The Beach Babes all thought it was really good idea, and so original. Poppy and Honey just couldn't believe they were part of it. The dance part gave them much more to do than before. Poppy felt like the luckiest girl in the world.